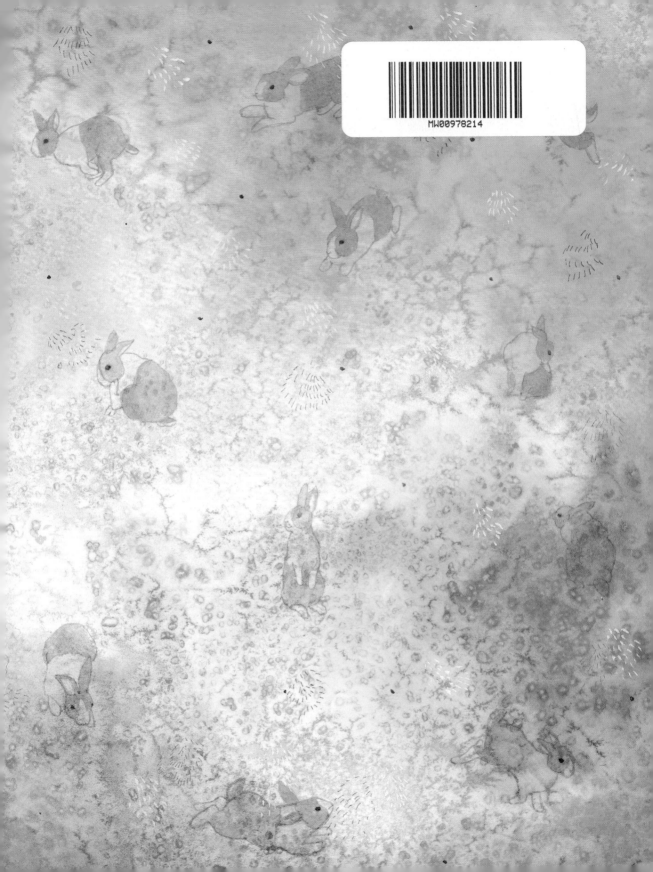

For Ella Telford and Sue McCrone

Text and illustrations copyright © Helen Cooper 1990

First American edition published 1990 by
Crocodile Books, USA
An imprint of Interlink Publishing Group, Inc.
99 Seventh Avenue • Brooklyn, New York 11215

Ella and the Rabbit was conceived and produced by
Frances Lincoln Ltd, Apollo Works
5 Charlton Kings Road, London NW5 2SB

Library of Congress Cataloging-in-Publication Data
available
Card Catalog # LC 90-34499

ISBN 0-940793-62-8

Printed and bound in Hong Kong

Ella
and the
Rabbit

Helen Cooper

Crocodile Books, USA

An imprint of Interlink Publishing Group, Inc.
NEW YORK

Ella's daddy had a champion rabbit. He had won a great golden cup in a special rabbit show.

If Daddy was with her, Ella was allowed to stroke him. The rabbit wrinkled his nose at Ella and blinked his big brown eyes.

Ella thought he was lovely.

One day Ella woke up very early, when the sky was pink and fluffy just like the rabbit's ears. She wondered if he was awake yet.

Ella quickly dressed, and crept outside to look at him. Only to look, only to say hello. That wouldn't be naughty, would it?

The rabbit lived in a hutch, inside a shed.
When he saw Ella he wrinkled his
velvety nose.
Ella longed to stroke his silky ears through
the wire. Only for a moment. That wouldn't
be naughty, would it?
She stroked him with her fingertips. He
looked as cuddly as could be. Surely it
wouldn't be naughty to open the door a
tiny bit?

So she did.
But then!
Quick as a wink the rabbit whizzed, out of
the hutch, and out of the shed.

"Oh no!" said Ella. "If Daddy finds out
he'll be mad. I must catch him quickly!"
The rabbit raced across the yard. He
stopped in front of the lawn mower, and
nibbled a dandelion.

Ella crept across the yard . . . and grabbed
him. But the rabbit squiggled and squirmed
out of Ella's hands and jumped over the
lawn mower.

By now the sun was high and golden in
the sky.
Daddy would be getting up soon.
She must catch that rabbit!
The rabbit jumped onto the wheelbarrow,
knocking flower pots everywhere.

Next he skipped along a flower bed.
Perhaps she could chase him back to
his hutch!
Round and round ran the rabbit. And
round and round ran Ella.
The flowers looked a bit squashed.

Ella picked up the net
from the strawberry
plants. Perhaps she
could throw it over him.
But somehow Ella got
the net all tangled round
herself.

The rabbit hip-hopped down the garden steps, and squeezed through a hole under the fence! Upstairs Daddy's alarm clock jingled and jangled!

In the field the rabbit sat and scratched.
But then . . . from the corner of his eye . . .
he saw an enormous marmalade cat,
looking straight at him.

The marmalade cat licked his lips!

And the rabbit bolted back,
under the fence,
up the steps,
along the flowerbed,
onto the wheelbarrow,
over the lawn mower,
across the yard,
into the shed . . .

and into his hutch!
Ella slammed the door
shut, just as Daddy
arrived.
"Hello Daddy,"
said Ella.